The Barley Sugar Ghosts

Nobody tells Nell that her grandmother's old barley sugar tin is full of valuables, so when she is helping out at the market stall one Saturday she sells it to a man in a big black hat. When she realises her mistake, Nell sets out with her brother Barney to find the tin. Things aren't that simple, however. Black Logan refuses to hand it over until the children find him some barley sugar, which he needs for a very important experiment, but there is a strike at the barley sugar mill. . . .

Hazel Townson is the author of several children's books. She lives in Lancashire, where she is Schools Librarian for the Metropolitan Borough of Bury, and her particular interests are amateur dramatics and local history.

The Barley Sugar Ghosts

Hazel Townson

Illustrated by Val Biro

Beaver Books

First published in 1976 by
Hodder & Stoughton Children's Books
47 Bedford Square, London WC1B 3DP

This paperback edition published in 1978 by
The Hamlyn Publishing Group Limited
London · New York · Sydney · Toronto
Astronaut House, Feltham, Middlesex, England
Reprinted 1980

© Copyright Text Hazel Townson 1976
© Copyright Illustrations
The Hamlyn Publishing Group Limited 1978
ISBN 0 600 31417 0

Set, printed and bound in Great Britain by
Cox & Wyman Limited
Reading
Set in Monotype Baskerville

Contents

1 *The missing casket*

It was market Saturday and Gran Porter trundled off with her barrow as usual, muttering to herself as she tried to keep the load of odds-and-ends from spilling. Antiques, Gran called her wares; but jumble was a better description. For she sold all the stray items she could find in her own rambling old house and in the houses of her neighbours. Odd cups and saucers, candlesticks, pictures without frames and frames without pictures, lidless pans, dusty wax fruit and even dustier books.

Her grandson Barney staggered along beside her, carrying an extra bundle which would not fit on the barrow. With him for her very first market-day, was his young sister Nell. Nell usually went to dancing school on Saturdays; ballet in the morning and ballroom in the afternoon, with luncheon at Miss Frogmore's in between. But today Miss Frogmore was sick, so there was no dancing school. Nell was delighted, for she had always envied her brother his regular Saturday trips to the market, especially since Gran always paid Barney a proportion of the day's takings. Gran, however, was not so delighted. She thought Nell would be in the way and an extra responsibility. Girls were all right in the house (Gran had to admit that Nell did her share of the cooking, washing-up and cleaning very well indeed) but they didn't know anything about business.

Gran stopped and beckoned impatiently to Nell.

'Come on, then, if you're supposed to be helping. Walk alongside and stop 'em toppling!'

She indicated the mountainous load of jumble, shifting, rattling and bumping along the rutted lane. The only item not shifting, rattling and bumping was Gran's Casket, for that was in its usual safe spot at the bottom of the pile.

Gran Porter's Casket was really just an old barley sugar tin, but it contained all her valuables ... a ring, a gold locket, a ruby brooch, her savings and important documents. Gran did not trust banks. And the Casket travelled everywhere with her because she would never leave it behind in the rambling old house in case of burglars.

Barney knew all about the Casket and had a proper respect for such an important item, but he had never mentioned it to Nell because Gran Porter had told him that the Casket was a secret.

'I don't want it talked about. If nobody knows it's there then they won't steal it, will they?'

So, since she knew nothing about it, how could Nell be blamed for selling the Casket to a perfect stranger before she had been at the market half an hour?

Gran and Barney were still busy setting

out the stall when the stranger walked
quietly up to Nell and asked if she sold
barley sugar. Nell remembered seeing the
barley sugar tin in the bottom of the
barrow, fetched it, tried in vain to open the
lid, and when the stranger impatiently
offered her a pound for the lot she took it.
A whole pound for a battered tin of barley
sugar! How clever she had been!

At the first opportunity, Nell boasted to Barney:

'Guess what a good piece of business I've just done! I got rid of that battered old barley sugar tin for a pound.'

Nell expected praise, and could not understand why Barney looked so stricken.

'You don't mean the Casket?'

'Oh, no; it wasn't a Casket,' Nell assured him blithely. 'Just an old tin with a dent in the side and scratches on the top, and the lid was so stuck I couldn't get it off.'

Barney groaned. 'That *is* the Casket, and it's full of all Gran's valuables. Oh, you prize idiot! Who bought it?'

'I'm NOT a prize idiot!' Nell retorted crossly. 'How was I to know what was in it? Anyway, it's too late now.'

'It had better not be. If we don't get that Casket back we'll be in more trouble than you ever dreamed of.'

Barney said 'we' because he always stood by his young sister in times of trouble. But he also said it because he was very fair-minded and could see Nell's point about not knowing. He ought to have warned her about the Casket, so it was partly his fault as well.

'A man in a black hat bought it,' Nell said sulkily.

'Which way did he go?'

'That way!' She pointed up the hill, away from the village.

Barney grabbed his sister's hand and began to drag her away from the stall.

'Come on, then! We've got to catch up with him.'

Gran Porter was busy haggling with a customer and did not see them go. By the time she looked up they were lost in the market crowd.

At first Gran supposed that Nell was bored or sick or something, and that Barney had taken her home.

'Might have told me, all the same,' she muttered, vowing not to give Barney any wages at all if he wasn't back at his post inside ten minutes.

But Gran's mild annoyance turned to furious panic when a little while later she discovered that the Casket was missing.

'Why, they've run off with it to tease me, the rapscallions! They've stolen it, that's what they've done! And me both father and mother to the pair of them since they was orphan babies.'

Gran poured out her troubles to Georgie Plum at the fruit stall next to hers. Georgie was sympathetic. 'Ah, children ain't what they was, and that's a fact. No gratitude, they haven't; not a scrap of it! Cut 'em a slice off an apple to taste, and they comes back when you're not looking and pinches your peaches.'

'I'll catch 'em, don't you fret!' Gran promised. 'And when I do I'll give 'em something to remember!'

Gran asked Georgie Plum's wife to keep an eye on her stall until she got back. Then, pausing only to pocket the takings, she bustled off in search of the children.

So there was Gran Porter chasing after Nell and Barney, who in turn were chasing after the man who had bought the Casket. And the man who had bought the Casket was none other than the villainous Black Logan himself.

2 *Black Logan's secret*

Everyone knew Black Logan was a villain because he looked like one. Ever since he had arrived on the scene a short time before, he had worn a hat with a wide, black brim, a pair of dark spectacles, a great untidy black beard and a turned-up coat collar.

'Shifty!' the villagers sniffed. 'Can't look you in the eyes and daren't let you see his face. We all know *his* sort!'

No one had ever actually caught Black Logan at his villainy, but if a chicken disappeared or a purse was lost or a windowpane was broken, then everyone knew Black Logan had passed by.

Barney knew Black Logan's reputation, but he was no more afraid of the villain than he was of telling Gran Porter that her

Casket was lost forever. So when Nell cried, 'There! That's him!' and pointed to Black Logan hurrying off into the woods with the Casket under his arm, Barney said stoutly:

'Right, then our troubles are nearly over. You wait here while I go and buy back the Casket.'

Flourishing the pound which he had thoughtfully brought with him for that very purpose, Barney ran after Black Logan.

Nell watched until both of them had disappeared into the woods, then she sat down on a stone, wishing she had never even heard of market day, and wondering if the whole thing wasn't after all Miss Frogmore's fault. If Miss Frogmore had not been sick, then Nell would have gone to the dancing school and none of this would have happened.

Barney found it gloomy in the woods. The footpath twisted and turned and at first he could not see Black Logan. He could hear him, though, and followed the sound as fast as he could, not caring how much noise he made himself.

Black Logan did not notice he was being followed. He strode on at a fast pace until he came to a cottage right in the middle of the wood. Not much of a place; just a plain, wooden, one-storey building with a couple of windows, a door and a chimney. Black Logan took out a key, unlocked the door and went inside, closing it carefully behind him. A few seconds later Barney ran up to the door and knocked loudly on it.

'Mr Logan, are you there? I've something important to tell you.'

Black Logan either did not or would not hear.

Barney ran to one of the windows and peered inside. He saw a simple living-room with a table and chairs, a fireplace, a sink, a stove and a cupboard. There was nobody there. He ran to the second window and stared into a bedroom which had nothing but a bed and a chair in it, except for a pair of boots on the floor and a few clothes hanging behind the door. Still nobody there. But Black Logan had gone inside; Barney had seen him. Was there something peculiar going on? Mystified, he ran right around the house in case there was another door at the back, but there was only one door.

Had Black Logan disappeared? Was he mixed up in some magic?

Barney felt uneasy. He began to doubt the wisdom of coming here alone. Perhaps he ought to go back to Gran while the going was good, and own up about the Casket. If he worked hard all his life he might be able to replace all the valuables.

Suddenly Barney noticed two things: first the Casket, sitting snugly on top of the cupboard, and second, the fact that the living-room window was open a crack at the bottom. Having tried the door already and found it locked, Barney decided to climb in through the window, take the Casket and leave the pound on the table with a scribbled explanation.

It was not an easy decision. Only the thought of Gran Porter, whom Barney regarded with a mixture of fondness and fear, could have driven him into that eerie house.

Gently he lifted the window a few inches higher and levered himself expertly over the sill. What he did not see until it was too late was the square, black, yawning hole in the floor right underneath the window. With a shout of dismay, Barney fell right into it.

There were steps in the hole, stone steps leading down from an open trapdoor to a dimly-lighted cellar. Barney bumped and slithered helplessly right down to the bottom step, where he came to rest in an undignified position, bruised and dirty but not seriously hurt. For a moment he lay there, collecting his wits, his courage and his breath. As his eyes grew accustomed to the gloom he could see a long bench with a lot of flasks and test-tubes and other things used in chemical experiments. Somewhere off to the left, in a patch of deep shadow, he could hear some gluey liquid bubbling.

It was from this patch of shadow that Black Logan suddenly emerged. He looked very frightening.

'Now you see what happens to breakers-in!' he said. 'First they get hurt and then they get caught.'

At the word 'caught' Black Logan shot out a long, black-sleeved arm and grabbed

Barney by the collar, dragging the boy to his feet. The black beard and spectacles moved closer to Barney's face.

'What are you up to, eh?'

Barney wished he could see Black Logan's eyes to find out how cross he really was. Still, he spoke up bravely, apologising for his sudden appearance, but pointing out that he had knocked loudly at the door.

'You followed me, didn't you?'

'Well, yes, I – I did.' Barney explained that the Casket had been sold by mistake, and offered Black Logan the money to buy it back. He hadn't much hope, of course. Either Black Logan already knew about the valuables in the Casket, in which case he wouldn't be likely to part with them again; or he'd be overjoyed at his luck. But Barney was in for a surprise. Black Logan reacted in quite a different way. He actually sounded upset.

'You mean to say there's no barley sugar in that tin?'

Barney agreed that there was not.

'But I heard it rattle! No barley sugar at all? Not a solitary piece?'

When the truth of this finally struck home, Black Logan threw himself on to a stool and clutched his head in an agony of despair.

'*Now* what shall I do? That was my very last chance!'

'I could try to get you some if you are all

that fond of it,' Barney offered. 'Only it isn't easy just now. There's a strike at the barley sugar mill.'

'Don't I know it?' Black Logan moaned. 'I've been everywhere – EVERYWHERE! – to try to get some, and just when I thought I'd found it . . .'

'You could try liquorice or aniseed balls or monkey nuts instead. They are all very nice.'

'You don't understand! It has to be barley sugar. I need it for my experiment; a vital experiment to put right another experiment that went wrong. Barley sugar is the main ingredient and I haven't a scrap of it.'

'Oh, I see.'

'No, you don't see!' cried Black Logan, leaping up and removing his hat, his dark glasses and his beard (which proved to be false) all in one swift movement.

'Look at my face! I invented this marvellous stuff called sun-tan oil, which I'm sure nobody has ever thought of before.

You spread it on your skin and sit out in the sun, and your skin turns a beautiful golden brown. It could have started a fashion, an absolute rage. It could have made me a fortune when I sold it on the market. But I tried it on my face, and look at me!' He picked up a lamp and held it close to his cheek. Barney stepped forward through the gloom to look – and gasped with horror. For Black Logan's face was a hideous bright green, with turquoise warts and whiskers.

'Won't it come off?' croaked Barney, goggle-eyed.

'Not unless I find some BARLEY SUGAR!' Black Logan almost screamed.

3 *The treasure in the tree*

Nell sat on the stone where Barney had
left her, sulking a little because she had
missed not only her dancing school but her
first day at the market, and quite likely her
lunch as well. Barney was a long time away.
Nell grew bored and had almost decided
to go back home and wait for Barney there
when she heard a voice behind her. It was
Gran Porter, hurrying towards her across
the field. Gran looked hot and furious.
Shaking her fist in the air, she shouted to
Nell to come here at once. Nell felt that she
could not do any such thing. To approach
an angry Gran Porter without the Casket
would be like telling a hungry lion you'd
bring him something to eat tomorrow. So
Nell ran off towards the woods.

Once she was among the trees, though, it occurred to Nell that she had not ventured into the woods by herself before, and might easily lose her way. It would be much simpler to climb a tree and hide until Gran had gone.

Nell was not very good at climbing, but necessity spurred her on. She picked the biggest tree she could find, jumped up to catch at the lowest branch, swung herself up to that and was away into the thick, dark foliage long before Gran appeared.

There was one nasty moment when Gran stood right under the tree, peering round to see which way Nell had gone, but she never thought of looking upwards. All the same, after that scare Nell felt she ought to climb higher, just in case.

Having climbed very high indeed, Nell stopped for breath. Clinging hard to the branch she was on, she began to look around her, and the first thing she saw was a great, golden eye winking down at her from a niche in the tree-trunk just above

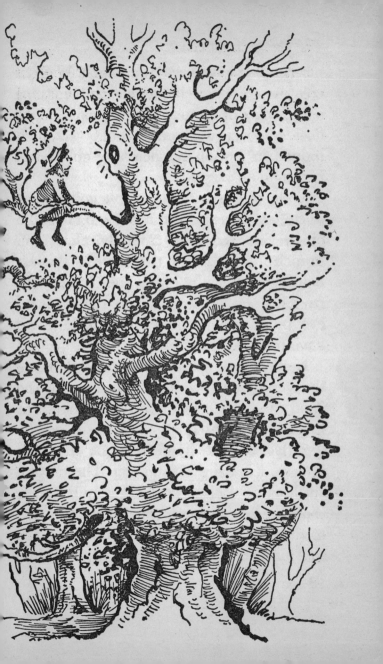

her head. It gave her quite a turn. Was it a creature – a squirrel or an owl or something – peering out from its hiding-place? Nell decided not; it was some sort of object, half-hidden in its hollow, gleaming gold when it caught the light.

Well, of course, Nell wasn't going to sit so close to treasure and not try to take hold of it. She wriggled carefully along her branch towards the tree trunk. Bravely holding on with only one hand, she stretched up an arm towards the golden eye, but it was just out of reach. She would have to stand up on her branch.

Nell was sitting astride the branch, facing the trunk. She lifted her left foot and placed it on the branch in front of her. Then she lifted her right foot, but misjudged it slightly so that it bumped against the branch, knocking her shoe off. There was a rustling, tumbling, crashing sound as the shoe hurtled down through the branches to the ground below. Horrified, Nell made the mistake of looking down after it and, seeing for the first time how high she had come, she completely lost her nerve.

Her head beginning to spin, Nell dropped back into her sitting-astride position and clung trembling to the branch. A chill dampness crept over her forehead and neck. What should she do now? She could not move for fright. And anyway, how could she climb down the tree without her shoe?

'I shall have to stay here for ever,' thought Nell in a panic. 'But I'll get tired and fall asleep, and then I'll let go of the branch and tumble.'

She imagined herself falling down through branch after leafy branch as the shoe had done, and she almost began to cry. She had to bite her lip very hard to keep back the tears.

Hours seemed to pass, though in fact it was not so very long, before a voice called out below:

'Nell! Nell, where are you?'

It was Barney. Hurrying back through

the woods from Black Logan's house he had caught sight of Nell's shoe lying under the tree.

'I'm here, right up the tree. Can you see me? Oh, Barney, I daren't come down.'

'Don't worry. Just sit still and I'll come up and get you.'

Nell felt dizzy with relief. Barney would rescue her. Barney would make everything all right. Realising now how much she relied on Barney and how good he always was to her, Nell vowed at that moment to be good to him as well. She would take all the blame for the missing Casket, and whatever trouble it involved she would try her best to get it back if Barney hadn't done so.

The rescue operation was not easy. Barney climbed up the tree with Nell's shoe in his pocket. Then he had to put it on for her whilst he himself balanced precariously on the branch below. Finally he had to guide her down the tree, coaxing and bullying her all the way and sometimes moving her feet with his hands. They were both worn out by the time they reached the ground, and Nell had forgotten all about the golden eye in her relief at being saved.

'You saved my life!'

'Rubbish! You'd have come down quick enough when you got hungry.'

'I *was* hungry.'

'Here, then, have a bit of chocolate,' offered Barney, unwrapping the sticky remains of a bar that he had found in his pocket.

At last Nell remembered to ask, 'Did you find the Casket?'

'I know where it is,' replied Barney. He explained about Black Logan's sun-tan oil and his horrible bright green face with turquoise warts and whiskers. 'He won't let me have the Casket back until I take him some barley sugar, and I must say I don't blame him. If I had a face like that I'd not want to go out shopping.'

'But the barley sugar mill is closed because the workers are on strike.'

'I know,' said Barney gloomily. 'The

shops have sold out whatever stocks they had and there just won't be any more until the strike is settled.'

Nell sat up suddenly. 'All right then, we'll settle the strike!'

Barney stared at his sister as if she had gone mad.

'Settle the strike? How on earth do you think we can manage that? We don't know the first thing about it.'

'Then we'll find out. We know where the mill is, and right next door to it is Tom Sweet's house. He's the owner of the mill, so he ought to know why the strike started. Let's go and ask him.'

'But Nell, we can't just do that . . .'

'Can you think of a good reason why not?'

Barney couldn't, so off they went. Nell's adventure in the tree was already forgotten, for at present there were more important things to think about.

4 *The Stick of Honour*

Tom Sweet had a rather fine house by the side of his barley sugar mill. The house was on top of a hill, with a view of three counties on a clear day, and a flagpole in the garden. But just now Tom took no pleasure in his fine surroundings. For the hum of the mill had long been silent, and there was no knowing when business would start up again. He was losing hundreds of pounds a week and was powerless to do anything about it. Gaunt and scowling he paced up and down his pathway, thinking thoughts so fierce that they almost struck sparks from the pavings.

'It's growing chilly, dear. Why don't you come in?' his wife called kindly from the doorway, but Tom took no notice.

At last he spotted two figures coming up the hill – children. Trespassers? Vandals? Flourishing his walking-stick he made his way towards them.

'What d'you want? This is private property, you know.'

Nell spoke up boldly, telling Tom right
away that they had come to help him settle
the strike.

Tom Sweet was dumbfounded. 'Help me
settle the strike? But you're only kids.
You don't know anything about it.'

'Well, the people who *do* know haven't
settled it, so we may as well try,' Barney
pointed out.

'If you can just tell us how it all started,
then we can put our brains to work,' said
Nell.

'Well, I'm blowed!' Tom Sweet scratched his head in sheer bewilderment. But he smiled all the same. You never knew, there might be something in it. As the boy said, everything else had failed, so why not try?

'Well, it was like this . . .' he began, finding it a relief to discuss the matter with somebody who didn't get all hot and bothered.

Tom went on to explain that his father, who had owned the factory before him, had started a scheme called the Stick of Honour Presentation. A solid gold barley sugar stick, worth hundreds of pounds, was given every tenth year to the firm's best worker. Two months ago it should have been presented to Aggie Meek, who had twisted with her own hands (plus, of course, the absolutely germ-free twisting-tongs) no less an average than 349 sticks of barley sugar every week for the last ten years.

'But on the night before the presentation the solid gold trophy disappeared and hasn't been seen again,' concluded Tom. 'The workers refused to work unless the presentation was made, but I didn't see why I should have to provide another Stick of Honour, especially since I thought one of them must have taken it.'

Nell looked thoughtful. Something gold stolen and hidden for two months? Why, there was something gold in the tree she had climbed, and up to now she had forgotten all about it.

'I think I know where the Stick of Honour is,' she suddenly exclaimed.

'Well now, if we can lay hands on that,' said Tom Sweet when she had told her story, 'we shall really be getting somewhere.'

'I'll go right back and fetch it,' offered Barney, but Tom would not hear of this. 'You must have some refreshments first,' he insisted. 'A sort of celebration. Then I'll go with you myself. You can show me which tree it's in and I'll do the climbing.'

Tom called out to his wife to tell her the good news. She was so overjoyed she made quite an occasion of it, producing chicken pasties and strawberry tarts and apple pie and cream, not to mention home-made trifle. Seated at a table by an open window, the children ate heartily, discussing all the time the treasure in the tree and the settling of the strike.

What they did not know was that they were being overheard by the local hero, Harry Hobble, who was outside the window doing a bit of weekend gardening for the Sweets.

Harry Hobble was every inch a hero. You had only to look at his open, honest face, his hard-working hands and the polish on his boots. Harry was the foreman at the barley sugar mill, and a fine, conscientious foreman he was, too. Always arrived five minutes early, and never coughed over the barley sugar mixture. Harry Hobble had given the best years of his life to Sweet's Barley Sugar Mill, as a proper hero should. Because of this he felt that he should have been chosen to receive the Stick of Honour instead of Aggie Meek, who, let's face it, did not have to use her brains at all from morning to night. She just kept on twisting and twisting. Harry, on the other hand, was a maker of decisions. Was the mixture too hot or too cold? Was there enough sugar in it? Was it being stirred at the right speed? And were the twisters twisting, or were they reading comics and swopping stamps and telling jokes behind Harry's back? Harry Hobble had been very much put out at not being offered the Stick of Honour, and had thought it only right that he should therefore steal that troublesome object and then quietly suggest a strike.

Now, as Harry hoed the border under Tom Sweet's dining-room window, he heard that his hiding-place had been discovered, though so far the golden Stick of Honour was still there. Flinging down the hoe, he made off at a furious pace towards the woods.

5 *Locked in the mill*

Harry Hobble was already halfway up the tree before Tom Sweet and the children had left the house. Having climbed the tree before, Harry knew every foothold and moved swiftly and surely towards his goal. What he did not know was that Nell's acrobatics as she had tried to reach the gold had seriously damaged the topmost branch. When Harry put his weight on it there was a terrible rending sound, the branch broke from the tree, and Harry, grabbing the Stick of Honour at the very last minute, was flung out like a broken toy. Down crashed Harry, taking other branches with him, until he reached one branch much stouter than the rest which caught hold of his trouser-seat and held him there, suspended in an unheroic pose just ten feet from the ground.

He was still there when Tom Sweet and the children arrived, so of course they had to rescue him, and he, in turn, had to offer some explanation. He said he had heard them talking about the Stick of Honour, and had wanted to be first up the tree to bring it down. Then, in true hero fashion, he handed it over with a flourish to his employer. Right then, it never occurred to any of them to ask Harry how he knew which tree to climb.

'The strike is settled, then!' cried Tom Sweet happily. 'Off you go, Harry my lad, and tell everyone to be back at work first thing tomorrow.'

'But tomorrow's Sunday,' Nell observed.

'So it is! Well, Monday morning, then. I can hardly wait that long.' Tom danced a jig under the tree, flinging his hands and feet about in the most ungentlemanly fashion, and Harry Hobble sped off to do his master's bidding.

Or so it had seemed at the time. What Harry did, in fact, was to hurry straight to the mill and lock himself inside it. Then he began to barricade the door with benches, chairs, tool-boxes, anything he could find. After that, he climbed up to all the windows and nailed planks across them to stop anyone getting in that way. When all his preparations were completed Harry looked round in satisfaction. Nobody could get in here on Monday morning, or any other morning, until Harry chose to let them in. He may have lost the first round of the battle, but he was not going to lose the second.

It was some time before Harry realised that he had forgotten to bring provisions for his siege. He could have done with a pillow and some blankets, but the worst mistake was food. He hadn't brought anything to eat.

'They'll starve me out!' he thought.

Then he remembered the barley sugar ingredients, packed to the ceiling in the store-room. Lighting a fire underneath the biggest vat, he poured in some water and began to measure sugar into it.

Meanwhile, Tom Sweet sent Nell and Barney home to explain to Gran Porter that she would have her Casket back on Monday, when the first batch of barley sugar was completed. Then he ran home to tell his wife the wonderful news.

Mrs Sweet met her husband at the gate.

'Look!' she shouted, pointing at the mill chimney which was smoking merrily, 'They've started work again!'

Tom was overjoyed. 'It's Harry Hobble, such a keen lad! Perhaps I should give him the Stick of Honour next time.' He made his way quickly to the mill to congratulate his foreman on the promptness of his action. But the mill doors were locked.

'Harry, it's me! It's Tom Sweet! Let me in, Harry lad! I've come to shake you by the hand.'

After a lot of useless banging and shouting, Tom went around to the windows one by one and tried to peer inside his mill. Suddenly it dawned on him that Harry meant to keep the workers out. Dismayed, he began to put two and two together. Harry listening in at the window; Harry knowing which tree to climb; Harry making off with the Stick of Honour – if he hadn't just happened to get caught up on a branch . . .

'It's treason! It's fraud! It's daylight robbery!' Tom yelled, chasing helplessly round and round the mill, pausing every now and then to shake a fist at a boarded window.

Inside the mill, Harry Hobble began to laugh. The first batch of barley sugar was all ready and cooling, so that soon he would have a nice, sticky supper to eat. As for a bed, he had spread sacks on the floor, which was warm from the boiling vat, and was sure he would be perfectly comfortable. He could stick it out for days, weeks, months, maybe even years.

6 *Plots and plans*

Tom Sweet felt he had nobody to turn to. He was worse off now than he had been during the strike, for there had always been a chance of that being settled some day. Now, with Harry Hobble locked in the mill, nothing was settled. Short of an earthquake, Tom could think of no way to get Harry out of there.

At last in desperation he decided to consult Barney and Nell. After all, they were the only ones so far who had done anything to help. Perhaps they would have some more bright ideas.

Off went Tom to Gran Porter's house, where he was received with some suspicion.

'What you done with my Casket, then?' demanded Gran, scowling round the half-open door.

Tom tried his best to explain all that had happened. It was just as well he did, for Nell and Barney, both talking at once, had mixed Gran up so much that she was completely bewildered.

When Gran was sure that Tom was a friend she let him in. Then he explained about Harry locking himself in the mill and the children were horrified.

'Why, that means we won't have our barley sugar after all,' cried Barney.

'And I won't get my Casket back!' shrieked Gran.

'And poor Black Logan won't get his face back, either,' Nell reminded them. Then she had an idea.

'We've got to fetch Harry Hobble out of the mill, and I think I know how we can do it. We'll get Black Logan to haunt him. One sight of Black Logan's horrible green face and Harry will fight his way out.'

'Not a bad idea,' said Barney, 'except that we can't let Black Logan into the mill to do the haunting and he can't haunt through the windows; they are all boarded up.'

Nell's face drooped with disappointment.

'There's a secret passage from my house to the mill,' Tom said thoughtfully. 'It comes up inside a cupboard in the mill store-room and I don't think anyone knows about it but my wife and me. Trouble is, it's only big enough for children and midgets. A grown-up like Black Logan would get stuck in it.'

The children looked at each other.

'Only big enough for children?' repeated Barney.

'Are you thinking what I'm thinking?' Nell asked him. Barney smiled and nodded.

'Well, I'm thinking too, as it happens,' Gran Porter butted in. 'I'm two jumps ahead of you. If you imagine you're going to plaster your faces with that horrible sun-tan oil and turn yourselves green-with-turquoise-warts-and-whiskers just so you can haunt Harry Hobble, you'd better think again. I'll lock you in your bedroom until you come to your senses. It's bedtime anyway.'

A noisy argument followed, in which everyone shouted at once. Tom pointed out that there was no need to have green faces to frighten Harry when a few ghostly noises would do. Nell protested that the green would not have lasted because Black Logan knew how to make the cure as soon as he got the barley sugar. Barney demanded to know if they were all going to sit there and let Harry Hobble get away with it.

'No, we're not!' declared Gran at last. 'Only we're going to do things my way for a change. I've had a few ideas myself, and one of them is to lock you two safely in your bedroom until you calm down. Then I'm going out for a while, and Tom's going to sit in and see you don't escape.'

Gran Porter had a powerful will. When she made up her mind to do something there was no way of stopping her. So it came about that Nell and Barney really did find themselves locked in their bedroom, with Tom keeping guard on the landing.

'I don't do this often,' Gran explained
to Tom, 'but I can read their minds. If I
don't keep those two under lock and key
tonight, there's no knowing what mischief
they'll get into.' So saying, she sped off
with the bedroom key.

As soon as they were sure that Gran had
gone, the children began coaxing Tom to
let them out.

'Come on, Mr Sweet! Unlock the door!
We're wasting precious time.'

'I can't; your Gran has the key.'

'Break the door down, then.'

'I can't go about destroying other people's property. It's against the law.'

'Well, fetch the ladder from the shed in the garden and rescue us through the window,' shouted Nell.

'Do you know what your Gran would do to me . . . ?'

'Oh, come on, you're not afraid of a helpless old woman, are you?' called Barney.

'Anyway, it's your mill. If you don't want us to help you we won't bother. But if I were you and I knew where there were two children ready and willing to crawl through a secret passage to save me from ruin I know what I'd do.'

'So do I!' cried Nell in hearty support. 'And I'd do it right away before it was too late.'

Tom Sweet groaned. He sat down on the stairs and thought for a bit. Then he went out to fetch the ladder.

7   *Three attempts at escape*

Gran Porter was a great one for security. The door of the garden shed was hung with an enormous padlock which completely defeated Tom Sweet's efforts to open it. He pulled and tugged and struggled with the chain, but all to no purpose. He tried to pick the lock, but had spent far too law-abiding a life to be much good at that. All he managed to do was to break the blade of his penknife and three fingernails.

Tom found it maddening to peer in through the little window and see the ladder that he wanted propped there right in front of him. He could have picked up a stone and broken the window, but he didn't think the ladder would have fitted through it anyway.

At last Tom realised there was nothing else for it but to break down the bedroom door as Nell had at first suggested. Better be quick, too. Gran Porter might soon be back.

So Tom ran back into the house. He would be breaking the law, but surely his cause was just? He was settling a strike, giving people their jobs back, saving them from starvation. He could only hope Gran would see it that way.

Tom called out to the children, warning them to stand clear of the door. But those who have ever tried to batter down a locked door will know that it is not as easy as it looks. It may be all right for a couple of burly policemen or a champion wrestler in a really bad temper; but for an ordinary person like Tom Sweet it is very difficult indeed.

Tom kept on charging into the door with his shoulder. The door wobbled a bit, but that was all. Tom's runs became longer and longer. Sweat poured from his brow and his shoulder began to hurt. At last he moved so far backwards for a final run that he came right to the head of the staircase, missed his footing and toppled backwards with a cry of startled rage. Tom's fall made a terrible din as he bumped on every step. The children were scared, especially since Tom did not call out reassuringly to say he was all right.

'He must have knocked himself out, or something,' said Barney.

'Well, don't just stand there, then. We'd better escape on our own and help him before Gran gets back.'

Barney did not need to ask how, for Nell was already stripping sheets from the two beds and knotting their corners together, as escaping heroes did in all the best stories.

Fastening one end of her rescue-line to the bed-post, Nell opened the window and began stuffing sheets frantically through it.

'Here, I'll go first,' said Barney. 'You know you don't like heights.'

Nell did not care to be reminded of her adventure in the tree. Secretly she was

dreading having to climb out of the upstairs window. In the end, though, it was the time of day that saved her, for by now it was quite dark and there was not even a moon. Nell could see nothing, even if she looked down.

Barney sat astride the window-sill. He, too, had uncomfortable memories of the window-sill at Black Logan's house and the surprise drop underneath it. He could only hope that things would go better this time.

Things did go better. Barney reached the ground safely with Nell not far behind him. Then, leaving the spoiled sheets dangling, they ran round to the front door to see what had happened to Tom.

Tom lay in a heap at the foot of the staircase.

'Is he dead?' whispered Nell.

' 'Course he isn't dead. He's breathing,' said Barney scornfully. He advanced boldly.

Tom, as a matter of fact, was just beginning to come round from what he described as 'a bit of a daze'.

'I must have bumped my head,' he said, feeling it carefully and finding a fair-sized lump behind one ear. 'But I'm all right now.'

Helped by Barney, Tom struggled to his feet. At first he was full of apologies for letting the children down, and then it dawned on him that they were here, free after all.

'How did you manage it?'

But there was not time to explain, for sudden footsteps and the lifting of a latch warned them that Gran Porter was coming home.

'Quick!' hissed Barney. 'Out the back way!'

'Here, wait for me!' Tom staggered after the children. They were only just in time.

8 The secret passage

The secret passage began in Tom Sweet's drawing-room. There was an oak settle screwed to a panel in the wall, which swung open when a lever behind the grandfather clock was pressed. The children were delighted with this and kept on opening and closing the panel just for fun.

It was not quite so much fun to venture down the worn stone steps into the dark, cramped passage, but eventually, armed with candles, they set out. Nell had suggested putting flour on their faces since they had not any of the sun-tan oil, but Tom assured them they would soon be so dirty that the flour would be a waste of time.

How right he was! Nell thought she had never been in such nasty surroundings in her life. The dust made her eyes itch and her nose tickle, so that she thought she was going to weep and sneeze at the same time. Added to that was the lack of space. In no time at all they had to crawl on their hands and knees. Barney went first, of course; but Nell soon began to wonder whether that was not the best position, for she seemed to keep on finding Barney's foot pushed into her face.

'Half a minute! I've dropped my candle!' Nell had stopped crawling and was groping around trying to find the missing candle, which had now gone out.

'Oh, honestly!' Barney hissed impatiently.

He waited for a moment but Nell went on groping.

'Here, I'll turn round and shine my candle, but for goodness' sake hurry up!'

Barney wriggled round and immediately bumped his head on the low ceiling.

'Ouch! That hurt!' He tried to raise a hand to his head but found that he could not manage it. In fact, he could not move at all.

'I'm stuck!' he exclaimed unbelievingly. 'I can't move an inch.'

'Oh, no!' Nell sounded really frightened. 'Barney, what are we going to do?'

Barney thought for a minute. Then he told Nell to crawl backwards out of the passage and ask Tom to help.

Nell thought this would be difficult. 'The passage has been sloping downwards for ages, so I'd have to crawl upwards and backwards at the same time.'

'Well, if you'd rather we just sat here until we turned into a couple of skeletons . . .'

'Perhaps I could turn round. I'm not as big as you.'

Barney was alarmed. 'Don't you dare try it! If you stick as well we really will be in trouble.'

So Nell began to crawl backwards. She had not gone far when she put one knee on the candle she had lost and immediately rolled forward again down the passage. In fact, she could not stop herself. Her head butted Barney right in his middle and sent him downwards too.

'That's done it!' he shouted triumphantly. 'I've come unstuck!'

'Yes, but now your candle's gone out as well, and we can't see a thing.'

' 'Course we can! There's the crack of light underneath the cupboard door! We've arrived!'

Another few feet and the passage grew roomier. Then they were actually in the cupboard and able to sit up and start haunting.

'Oooooh! Aaaaaa! Whooooo! Wheeeee!'

Nell did not think they sounded much like real ghosts, but Barney fancied they were doing quite well. At any minute now Harry Hobble would hear them. He would either be scared to start with, or he would open the cupboard door to see what was making the noise. When he did that the children were ready to pounce and frighten

him out of his wits, disappearing back down the passage before Harry had worked out whether they were ghosts or humans or prehistoric monsters. He would not stay in the mill by himself after that.

Yet Harry did not open the cupboard door. As a matter of fact he was fast asleep and did not hear a thing.

After a great deal of most un-ghostly banging and shouting, the children finally realised they would have to crawl all the way back to Tom Sweet's house without having settled anything.

'What idiots we shall look. All that effort for nothing!'

'We've still to face Gran, as well. What do you think she'll say about the sheets?'

'She might not have noticed them,' said Barney with a confidence he did not feel. 'We'll take them down and wash them and she'll never know.'

'Well, all the same I hate that horrible passage. It's such a long way back.'

'Come on, cheer up! We've lit our

candles again now, and think how much worse we'd have felt if we'd plastered our faces with that awful sun-tan oil as well.'

But consolation had come too soon. As they turned to leave the cupboard the children suddenly discovered they were trapped. A secret panel at the back of the cupboard, built in to hide the entrance to the passage, had quietly closed whilst they had been busy haunting Harry.

Nell bit her lip, trying hard not to panic.

'Barney, what shall we do?' she whispered at last. Her voice sounded shaky but she was not going to cry.

'Don't worry; it'll be all right,' Barney reassured her. 'Let's just think for a bit.'

When he had thought he explained that they must have made the secret panel work by accident, by touching or treading on something. 'So all we have to do is to keep on repeating the movements we've made since we climbed into the cupboard.'

'Can't we just go out through the cupboard door? I don't care what Harry

Hobble says or does. I don't like being trapped in here.'

'I don't like it either, but we can't get out that way because the cupboard door is locked. And you know we've already tried hard enough to make Harry hear us. He's either fallen asleep or gone away.'

Nell took a deep breath. 'Well then, let's think of all the things we've done. We crawled in on our hands and knees, like this. Then we sat up, like this. Then we stood up, like this. Then we made all those funny moans and groans and I flung my arms about a bit, like this. And you made those scratchy noises on the wood.'

'Oh, yes, like this!' Barney was suddenly hopeful, but nothing happened.

'We must have done something else as well.'

'No, we didn't. I'm sure we didn't.'

'You scratched your head. I saw you.'

'Well, what difference would that have made, silly?'

There was another miserable silence. Then Barney had a fresh idea.

'Let's run our hands over every single bit of the walls and floor. We must have pushed a secret button or something. You start at that side and I'll start over here.'

Slowly and carefully the two children covered every inch of the inside of that cupboard with their eagerly searching fingers. Still, all that happened was that Nell ran a splinter into her thumb, and Barney's candle flickered and died while he was trying to take the splinter out.

'Oh, no!' cried Nell. 'Now we've only my candle left, and I don't suppose it will last much longer than yours.'

'Blow it out and save it to use when we're crawling back.'

'Blow it out?' Nell was horrified. 'But then it will be pitch black in here.'

'So what? If you shut your eyes you won't know the difference. Come on, Nell, we shall need that light later.'

'How *much* later?' Nell grumbled, obeying her brother all the same and shutting her eyes very tightly.

'Now then, sit down. We may as well be comfortable.'

'Aren't we going to do anything?'

'There is nothing else to do except think. Anyway, you needn't worry. When we don't arrive back at Tom's house he will guess there's something wrong. Then he'll rescue us.'

'But how? He's too big to crawl down the passage, and he must not have known about the panel or he would have told us.'

'I expect he just forgot to mention the panel,' said Barney, trying to keep his sister's spirits up. Yet deep down inside Barney had a feeling that things had gone very wrong indeed. For the moment he was completely stumped.

9 *A marble miracle*

Black Logan, too, had had to admit defeat.
He had spent half the night trying hard to
make his own barley sugar and the other
half trying to find a substitute for barley
sugar in the experiment that would put his
face to rights. Nothing had worked. It was
nearly dawn and he was quite worn out.
But he was not going to bed. Instead he
began to pack a rucksack for he had made
up his mind to flee. He would go away and
hide where nobody could find him. He
would become a hermit, living on berries
and roots and talking to himself. For Black
Logan could not bear to look so villainous
and ugly. He was sure he was the most
unpopular person in the world, and now
that Barney had found out where he lived

he would tell everyone, and they would all come along to laugh. Why, Black Logan might even be arrested for crimes he had not committed.

Up in the mountains there was a deserted stone hut that Black Logan had once come across. A tumbledown place, but he could build it up again. If Robinson Crusoe had managed then why shouldn't he? The thing was to take the right sort of tools, so that what you didn't have you could make. Black Logan began to search his tool-box carefully.

He did not intend to take any of the chemical apparatus with him. Black Logan was done with chemistry. Chemistry had been his downfall; the ruin of his face and his life. So disgusted was he with his tubes and flasks and crucibles that when he accidentally knocked over the flask containing the remains of his last experiment he did not even bother to pick it up. The flask held a dirty brown liquid which dripped slowly on to the floor.

When everything else was packed, Black

Logan searched his larder. He found potatoes, bananas, eggs, a packet of dates and half a loaf. There was also a bottle of ginger beer which he had been saving to drink a toast to the success of his experiment.

'Better take it all,' he decided. 'There won't be any shops where I'm going, and I may not be all that keen on roots and berries.'

At last all was ready. With a final, sad glance around, Black Logan turned to leave his basement. Then suddenly he stopped. Something had caught his eye. Something was gleaming on the floor. Puzzled, Black Logan went over to look. It was the pool of brown liquid which had dripped from the overturned flask. At least, it should have been a pool of brown liquid, but it wasn't. It was now set hard and gleaming, with the beautiful texture of finely-polished marble!

Could it be true?

'Instant floors!' Black Logan breathed. 'I've invented Instant Liquid Floors. It's never been heard of before! Oh, I'm ahead

of my time, and no mistake! Do-It-Yourself, Pour-On, No-Waiting, Sets-In-A-Jiffy Marble Halls! And statues! Why, I could dip lumps of carved wood into this stuff and they'd come out like marble busts.'

There was no end to the wonderful possibilities. Transformed with enthusiasm, he dropped his rucksack and feverishly began to test his precious product. It really worked! Finding a bit of paper, Black Logan hastily scribbled down the ingredients and method he had used to achieve the brown liquid in the first place. Was it one ounce of powdered dandelions, or two? Well, he would soon find out, for he intended to make some more at once. Lots more! Buckets and buckets of the stuff. Then he would bottle it and sell it on the market, and his fortune would be made.

'I'll start a fashion for Instant Floors! And that's only the beginning. If there can be Instant Floors, then why not Instant Walls, Potatoes, Gravy . . . Instant Everything?'

Black Logan had forgotten about his face. So absorbed was he in the marble miracle that it never once occurred to him that to sell this stuff on the market he would have to stand behind a stall where all could stare at him.

'A really good name – that's all I need now,' he pondered as he worked. 'A name that's easy to remember and looks well on a label.' Why not thump two words together into one? Marbyflor? Flickaflor? No, no; it wasn't just for floors, this wonderful stuff. It was for anything and everything.

'Instamarb? Marbadrip?'

Then all of a sudden it came to him in a shock of pure inspiration – SQUARBLE!

'*Turn everything to marble*
With a little squirt of Squarble!'

'Yippee!' cried Black Logan, throwing his hat, false beard and dark glasses up into the air. 'I'm famous! I'm a millionaire! I'm the pioneer of a brave new Instant world!'

He began to dance a hornpipe on his bit of marble floor.

Harry Hobble had a nice, long sleep on his sacks, and although he woke up feeling rather stiff he was pleased with himself for having managed things so well. A good, hot bath and a nourishing breakfast and he'd feel really fit. But of course there was no hot bath; not even a bit of soap to wash his hands and face with. What's more, the only breakfast he could look forward to was a stick or two of barley sugar, the very thought of which set his stomach lurching. Already he was heartily sick of the taste of barley sugar. Yet Harry was enormously hungry. He began to prowl around the mill, searching for odd scraps dropped from workers' lunch-boxes, but it was all too long since any workers had picnicked there.

Whatever crumbs they had scattered the mice had long since carried off.

Dreaming of eggs and bacon and fat, brown, sizzling sausages, Harry prowled right round to the front doors. And there he had a surprise. An exciting-looking package had been pushed through the letter-box. What's more, it was addressed to:

> The Foreman,
> Sweet's Barley Sugar Mill

so there was nothing to stop Harry opening it. It might even be a box of chocolates.

Hastily tearing away the wrappings, Harry soon held in his hands a bottle labelled: LIQUID SOAP.

'What a present!' snorted Harry in disgust. Nobody sane could eat that, nor even drink it. Such a disappointment! Harry was about to throw the bottle into the waste-bin when he remembered his earlier dreams of a lovely, hot bath. At least now he could wash his hands and face.

There was a sink in the corner of the Twisting Room. Harry ran some water into it and sprinkled it lavishly with liquid soap. Then he washed his face and dried it on his handkerchief, glancing up into the mirror to see if he looked any cleaner, or at any rate all sparkling-morning-fresh.

What Harry saw in the mirror made him gasp with horror! He began to tremble. He felt sick. He screeched. Then he screamed. Then he absolutely roared with panic. For his face was a hideous bright green all over, with turquoise warts and whiskers.

Too late did it dawn on our hero that today was Sunday, and that no proper postman would be delivering packages. Some villain had been lurking there outside. Some loathsome criminal had tried to murder Harry. For of course he *had* been murdered. He was bound to die. Who ever heard of anybody *living*, whose face was green with turquoise warts and whiskers? Utterly beside himself, Harry threw water at his face in violent handfuls, but the green

grew even greener and the turquoise warts increased in size. He grabbed a sugary sack and scrubbed his face with it, but that made matters even worse. The next time he looked in the mirror he was convinced that his head was growing bigger.

'It's going to explode!' he thought. 'I'm a living bomb!'

Well, in view of that, of course, Harry wanted nothing better than to escape into the open. He wanted to run and run until he found a doctor. Someone – anyone – who would help him. Feverishly he began to drag away the boxes and the furniture he had piled so carefully against the door.

'Let me out! Let me out!' he roared, as the structure started toppling all about him.

Meanwhile, Gran Porter had discovered by now that Nell and Barney were missing and had decided not to mind, for they were surely in Tom Sweet's good hands, though no doubt up to mischief. She it was, and not poor Harry, who sat down to the nourishing breakfast of eggs, bacon, and fat brown sizzling sausages.

Gran had decided not to mind about the children's escape because she knew now that they could not have been up to the worst piece of mischief with the sun-tan oil, for Gran herself had disposed of that. Hadn't she trudged all the way to Black Logan's house with the left-overs from her stall still in the barrow (a bunch of wax grapes, a nutmeg-grater, two pot dogs, a dozen assorted books and a box of dominoes) and exchanged all these priceless items for that terrible sun-tan bottle which she had quickly re-labelled 'LIQUID SOAP'?

11 *The barriers come down*

Tom Sweet looked at his watch. He shook it and held it to his ear. He checked it against the grandfather clock. Could all that time really have passed since the children crawled into the passage? It was quite unforgivable of him to have dozed off in the chair whilst he was waiting. Now something was wrong and he would have to act quickly.

Tom began to feel very guilty indeed about letting the children start out upon such a wild adventure. Gran Porter was quite right; the two of them should have stayed locked in their bedroom for the night. Well, he was the one who had helped them to escape. If only he had kept quiet about the secret passage! But it was too late now.

He must do something to save Nell and Barney.

Tom looked at himself in the mirror.

'I'm not all that big. I might just manage it.'

Lowering himself to his hands and knees he made a move towards the passage entrance, yet almost at once he could see that it was no use trying. Which meant he would have to tackle the problem from the other end. But it was no use trying to make Harry Hobble let him in, either. Tom could think of nothing else to try. So bothered and upset was he that he groaned as he paced aimlessly back and forth considering what to do.

He groaned so loudly that he woke up his wife who had been fast asleep for hours and knew nothing of the ghostly goings-on. Mrs Sweet came sleepily into the room in her dressing-gown.

'Whatever are you up to at this time of night?'

Poor Tom continued to groan, quite

distracted by his guilt and misery. There seemed nothing for it but to put the kettle on and make a nice cup of strong, sweet tea.

'Now,' said Mrs Sweet, forcing the teacup into Tom's unwilling hands, 'you'd better tell me all about it.'

So Tom did.

'H'm! I can't say you behaved with a great deal of sense, and goodness knows what Gran Porter will say when she finds out what's been happening. But I think I can help you all the same.'

'You can?' Tom leapt swiftly towards his wife, upsetting the cup of tea all over the carpet. Mrs Sweet pretended not to notice.

'I expect it's the secret panel. The children will have closed it by accident and won't know how to open it again.'

Tom struck his forehead in despair.

'Oh, why didn't I think to tell them?' he wailed. 'It completely slipped my mind in the excitement.'

'Don't worry. We can open the panel from this end just as well. There's that rusty

83

old lever behind the grandfather clock.'

'Of course, of course! It pulls the wire that runs right through the passage. I'd forgotten all about it.'

How eagerly Tom rushed to grasp that lever! And how eagerly Barney leapt up in the cupboard when he heard the panel moving!

'Nell! Quick, light your candle! Something seems to have worked.'

'What's worked?' Nell muttered sleepily, for she too had dozed off during the long wait.

'I don't know what, but we're free! Let's move out quickly before the panel closes again.'

Nell needed no second telling. She was through the gap into the passage before Barney had finished speaking.

'Now you've gone first,' Barney grumbled. 'You'll have to lead all the way and I won't be able to help you.'

'I don't care,' crowed Nell. 'Anyway, I've got the candle.'

'Well, don't drop it this time.'

Nell had been dreading the journey back through that cramped and dirty passage, but now she was so pleased to be inside it at all that she made wonderful progress and never even stopped to think how much farther there was left to crawl. Altogether it seemed a much shorter and less uncomfortable journey than the first one, and the children were soon struggling up towards the bright lights of Tom Sweet's drawing-room and the welcoming arms of his wife.

Tom Sweet stared at the filthy, bedraggled children as they crawled out of his secret passage. No need to ask if the haunting had worked; he could see at once that it had not. But of course all that mattered now was that the children were safe.

'Harry wouldn't open the cupboard,' Barney mumbled shamefacedly. 'I don't think he even heard us. It was locked on the outside so we couldn't get out.'

'The panel shut, too, and it was very

scary,' said Nell, quite proud now to have come through such an ordeal.

Tom tried his best to comfort them. Perhaps it was just as well they couldn't open the cupboard door, he said, for Harry might have turned nasty if he'd thought they were real ghosts.

'Harry Hobble turn nasty? But he's supposed to be a hero.'

'Haven't you learnt yet that heroes behave badly sometimes, just as villains do good turns now and then?'

'But Tom, we haven't settled your strike,' mourned Nell. 'What will happen now? Are you ruined?'

Tom patted her kindly on the shoulder. 'Don't you worry; it will all come out right in the end.'

Mrs Sweet, tutting at the sorry state the children were in, now bustled them off for hot baths and hot drinks whilst Tom gave their clothes a thorough brushing and shaking.

'Now then, put your things on again,'

said Mrs Sweet at last, 'and we'll take you back to Gran Porter's. Somebody will have to tell her what's been going on.'

At the thought of Gran's wrath to come the children's shoulders drooped. Yet there was no help for it; the worst would have to be faced. If only it hadn't all been in vain.

Suddenly there came the sound of a distant commotion. Something was happening at the mill!

Shouting and banging and crashing noises grew louder as the four of them stood listening. Then they all moved at once.

'It's Harry Hobble! Come on!'

Across Tom's garden they ran, through the dewy dawn. Excited as she was, Nell could not help thinking that it seemed much quicker running to the mill this way than crawling through the passage.

As they drew nearer to the mill they could see Harry Hobble clambering over heaps of broken furniture, like a Guy come to life on an unlit bonfire. He was throwing his arms about and shouting something desperate which they could not quite hear.

Then they saw Harry's face.

'It's the sun-tan oil!'

'No wonder he's frantic!'

'But how did he get hold of it?' (Quite a long time was to pass before they found out the answer to that.)

'I say, doesn't he look a sight? Even worse than Black Logan.'

Nell immediately felt sorry for Harry and ran after him to tell him that everything would be all right.

'Black Logan's face is the same,' she called, 'but he's making a cure. All he needs is some barley sugar, and then . . .'

But Harry did not seem to be listening.

'Help! I've been murdered!' he cried, dashing off down the hill as if there were bee-swarms after him. He ran so fast that

Nell thought he would never be able to stop. If he was not careful he would plunge straight into the river at the bottom of the hill.

But there were more shocks in store.

Tom, staring at the ruins of his mill furniture, had suddenly noticed smoke pouring out of the doorway. Harry had let the barley sugar vat boil dry and now the whole place was on fire.

'Help! Fire! Water! Quick!' cried Tom, running aimlessly back and forth in search of a bucket. 'The mill's on fire! Do you hear, Harry, the mill's on fire? You're the Foreman, so DO SOMETHING! HELP!'

Harry Hobble heard the desperate cry. Tom Sweet's panic got through to him beyond his own, and with a gigantic effort and a veering sideways Harry made himself slow down. He stopped. He paused. Then he turned and ran back up the hill to help Tom fight the fire.

Harry knew just where to put his hands on the fire-bucket, although he had to fight his way through the flames to do it. How hot it was! And how Harry gasped and choked on the nasty fumes! There was a horrible smell of burning metal and Harry guessed that the vat was gone for good. Still, they could always buy another vat as long as the mill was saved.

Funny how Harry had changed his tune. Now that the mill was in danger he realised how much he wanted to save it, to go on working there with his friends, spending his days making barley sugar to keep all the children happy. It was a good life. He couldn't think why he had wanted to spoil it all.

By the time Barney had fetched the fire-brigade, Harry already had the blaze under control, the danger was past and the mill was saved. What is more, so hard had Harry Hobble worked to bring this about that he stood before the firemen mopping his bright green face with its turquoise warts and whiskers and never even thought what a sight he must look.

12 *The presentation party*

It was a lovely sunny afternoon. From Tom Sweet's garden there was a fine view of three counties, and the Union Jack fluttered gaily from the flagpole. A garden party was in progress, at which the Guest of Honour was Aggie Meek, about to be presented with the Golden Stick of Honour.

The Stick of Honour, in its presentation case of scarlet leather, lay on a Squarble-topped table in the middle of the lawn, and the guests, at a sign from Tom, all gathered round it.

Tom made a speech, praising Aggie's devotion to duty and bringing a modest blush to that lady's cheeks. He handed her the Stick of Honour amid cheers and loud applause.

But to everyone's surprise Aggie Meek,

too, had something to say. She thanked her employer for the honour he had done her, but felt there was one better fitted to receive the trophy than herself. Who was it, she asked, who had saved the mill from burning in the midst of his own personal troubles? Who was the hero to end all heroes?

More cheers and more applause followed Aggie's handing over of the Stick of Honour to Harry Hobble.

Harry – positively scarlet with pride – said, too, how grateful he was, but reflected that there was one amongst them who had been grossly misjudged. Now and again, said Harry, things had gone wrong in the village. A purse was lost or a chicken disappeared or a window-pane was broken. Somebody had to be blamed. Somebody had to be cast for the part of villain. Yet the purse had been found, the chicken had only strayed up the lane, and the window-pane, it turned out, had been mistaken for a goalpost.

'Yet did we say we were sorry for our nasty suspicions? No, we did not. But we are jolly well going to do it now.'

People began to shuffle their feet and hang their heads with shame and mutter uneasily. They had all behaved badly and they knew it.

'You all know who I mean,' Harry continued, not sparing anybody's feelings. 'I mean Black Logan, without whose help I shouldn't be here today, turning my pink, healthy face to the crowd.' Black Logan, he concluded, was the real hero, patient, uncomplaining, brave and brilliantly inspired. Black Logan should have the Stick of Honour.

'Me?' cried Black Logan, thoroughly taken aback. Without his hat, beard, spectacles and turned-up collar, which of course he had no more need to wear, he looked quite as much a hero as Harry. But he did not feel like a hero. He had grown used to being thought a villain and the sudden change made him uneasy. He wanted to be rid of the Stick of Honour as quickly as possible, so he passed it to Nell and Barney, without whose help, he pointed out, he would have had no barley sugar anyway.

'Besides, I'm not a hero, I'm a coward. I nearly ran off to be a hermit.'

'We nearly drove you off, you mean,' interrupted Barney, 'so how can we accept the Stick of Honour? Anyway, come to that, if it hadn't been for our Gran Porter . . .'

But Tom Sweet silenced him.

'Look here,' said Tom, 'we can't spend all day passing this thing round from one person to another. If nobody wants it, then why don't we sell it and divide the money up between you all?'

'Good idea!' shouted Gran Porter. 'Who wants a golden barley sugar stick anyway? Dust-collector, that's all it is. Useless sort of object. Fit for nothing but a junk-stall on the market.'

Everyone began to laugh.

'Hear that? Got an eye for a bargain, has Gran Porter.'

'Ah, she's a sly one, she is!'

'Slyer than you'll ever know,' agreed Gran, winking mischievously at Nell and Barney behind Harry Hobble's back.

More Beaver Books

We hope you have enjoyed this Beaver Book. Here are some of the other titles:

The Beaver Book of the Seaside A Beaver original. Snorkelling and surfing, birdwatching and beachcombing – plus facts about ships, lighthouses, smuggling, wrecks and lots of other fascinating topics. A book for everyone who loves the seaside by Jean Richardson; illustrated by Susan Neale and Peter Dennis

The Sugar Trail Mystery Dan always notices things that other people don't think important, and when tools start disappearing from the local warehouse he is soon hot on the thief's trail. Written by Jean Wills and illustrated by Paul Wright for readers of six to ten

Cooking is Easy A Beaver original. Recipes for delicious meals for every time of day, plus suggestions for special occasions, presents and eating out of doors. Written by Jane Todd, Cookery Editor for the Hamlyn Group, and illustrated by Marilyn Day and David Mostyn

These and many other Beavers are available from your local bookshop or newsagent, or can be ordered direct from: Hamlyn Paperback Cash Sales, PO Box 11, Falmouth, Cornwall TR10 9EN. Send a cheque or postal order, made payable to The Hamlyn Publishing Group, for the price of the book plus postage at the following rates:
UK: 30p for the first book, 15p for the second book and 12p for each additional book ordered to a maximum charge of £1.29;
BFPO and EIRE: 30p for the first book 15p for the second book plus 12p per copy for the next 7 books, thereafter 6p per book;
OVERSEAS: 50p for the first book and 15p for each extra book.

New Beavers are published every month and if you would like the *Beaver Bulletin*, which gives a complete list of books and prices, including new titles, send a large stamped addressed envelope to:

Beaver Bulletin
Hamlyn Paperbacks
Banda House
Cambridge Grove
Hammersmith
London W6 0LE

314170